IT'S A MITZVAH, GROVER!

By Tilda Balsley and Ellen Fischer
Illustrated by Tom Leigh

KAR-BEN
PUBLISHING

For my niece Sloan and her three terrific guys – T.B

Dedicated with love to Jeanne, Liz and Scott – E.L.F.

For Sarah – T.L.

KAR-BEN PUBLISHING, INC.
A division of Lerner Publishing Group, Inc.
241 First Avenue North
Minneapolis, MN 55401 U.S.A.
1-800-4-Karben

Website address: www.karben.com

Library of Congress Cataloging-in-Publication Data

Balsley, Tilda.
    It's a mitzvah, Grover! / by Tilda Balsley and Ellen Fischer ; illustrated by Tom Leigh.
        p.   cm.
    Summary: Grover and Avigail join their friends Brosh and Mahboub to clean up a playground in Israel as a mitzvah, and although grouchy Moishe refuses to partici-pate, he finds his own way to make the world a better place.
    ISBN 978–0–7613–7562–3 (lib. bdg. : alk. paper)
    [1. Helpfulness—Fiction. 2. Commandments (Judaism)—Fiction. 3. Jews—Israel—Fiction. 4. Israel—Fiction.]
    I. Fischer, Ellen, 1947– II. Leigh, Tom, ill. III. Title.
    PZ7.B21385Moi 2013
    [E]—dc23   2012009497

Manufactured in the United States of America
1 – PC – 12/31/2012

Hello everybodeee!

It is I, your furry blue friend Grover, writing from Israel. I am going to tell you how my friends on Rechov Sumsum helped out with *tikkun olam*. That is Hebrew for making the world a better place.

Grover scratched his head. "Tee-kune what?" Grover was having a great time in Israel, but some of these Hebrew words were really tricky for a little blue monster.

"Tikkun olam," explained Brosh. "It means 'repairing the world.' The storm has made a mess of our playground. I think we should fix it up and make it even better than before."

Avigail clapped her hands. "Hooray! Avigail loves to help."

"Yes," said Mahboub. "First we're going to sweep and clean, and then we're going to paint the swings, slide, and seesaw."

"Because we're repairing the world, we're doing a *mitzvah*," said Brosh.

Grover scratched his head again. "A what?"

"A mitzvah," repeated Brosh. "It means to do something nice for others."

"Come with us," Avigail invited. "You'll see."

"I am coming!" said Grover, grabbing a broom.

Mahboub pulled the wagon of paint, and the friends headed off together to the playground.

They passed Moishe Oofnik's trash can on their way. "Hey Moishe," Brosh called. "We're fixing up the playground. It's a mitzvah, you know. How about helping us?"

"Forget it! I don't like helping, and I don't want to do a mitzvah," he said. "Too much time, too much trouble! Now scram!" He shut his trash can lid with a bang.

"Once a grouch, always a grouch," said Mahboub.

At the playground, they found all kinds of trash—a banana peel, a rotten falafel, a smelly tennis shoe. Everything went into trash bags. The friends swept the leaves off the slide, and they untangled the swings. With everyone helping, it didn't take long to clean things up.

"Let's start painting," said Brosh. "We have red, blue, and yellow paint. I'm going to use red, because I love apples, cherries, strawberries, and pomegranates."

"I've got yellow," said Mahboub, "like sunflowers, loquats, lemons, and grapefruit."

"Please pass the blue," said Grover. "Blue like the color of the sky, the ocean, and, of course, yours truly—adorable little me."

Avigail looked sad. "Oh," she said. "Avigail really wanted purple. Avigail loves grapes, plums, and purple hair ribbons. Purple makes Avigail happy."

"No problem," said Brosh. "Watch this, Avigail. We can mix red and blue to make purple."

"Be still, my little monster heart," said Grover. "Brosh, did you not just do a mitzvah for Avigail?"

Avigail giggled. "Yes, Avigail is happy!"

"Look," called Mahboub. "I mixed blue and yellow and made green— like avocados, kiwis, and zucchini.

And over here, I mixed red and yellow to make orange—like carrots and tangerines."

"Our playground will be so pretty," said Avigail, "just like a rainbow."

When they were all finished painting, Brosh said, "The playground looks great. But look at us, and look at all these bags of trash."

"I know what to do with the trash," said Mahboub. "Follow me."

They piled the bags into the wagon and headed down the street.

"Moishe, come out!" called Mahboub.

Moishe stuck his grouchy face out of the trash can. "What do you want?"

"Look what we brought you," said Mahboub, pointing to the garbage bags.

"Trash? For me?" asked Moishe.

"Yes," said Avigail. "We're doing a mitzvah."

Moishe grabbed a bag and looked inside. "What wonderful, awful trash—it's even got rotten food, my favorite.   Maybe a mitzvah for *oofniks* is not so bad."

Moishe reached into the bag and pulled out a soda can. "Wait a minute. This is not trash!" He tossed the can into a nearby recycling bin. "And this, and this, not trash, not trash."

"I cannot believe my monster eyes," said Grover. "Recycling is a mitzvah! Moishe, you are doing a mitzvah."

"Oh no," Moishe groaned, and he ducked back into his trash can. "I knew this was going to be a rotten day!"

"It's okay," Avigail called after him. "It's okay. You're still a grouch."

"And we're still a mess!" said Grover.
"Let's go wash up."

About the Authors and Illustrator

Tilda Balsley has written many books for Kar-Ben, bringing her stories to life with rhyme, rhythm, and humor. Now that *Sesame Street* characters populate her stories, she says writing has never been more fun. Tilda lives with her husband and their rescue Shih Tzu in Reidsville, North Carolina.

Ellen Fischer, not blue and furry, or as cute and loveable as Grover, was born in St. Louis. Following graduation from Washington University, she taught children with special needs, then ESL (English as a Second Language) at a Jewish Day School. She lives in Greensboro, North Carolina, with her husband. They have three children.

Tom Leigh is a longtime illustrator of *Sesame Street* and Muppet books. He lives on Little Deer Isle off the coast of Maine with his wife, four dogs, and two cats.